DESERT buddies
•life in a sunbaked land•

By
Dabney Miller Philabaum
and
Nancy Lenches Alegret

Second Edition Copyright © 1996
by Dabney Miller Philabaum and
Nancy Lenches Alegret for Earth Buddies

All Rights Reserved

Publisher's Cataloging in Publication
(Prepared by Quality Books Inc.)

Philabaum, Dabney Miller.
Desert buddies : life in a sunbaked land / written & illustrated
by Dabney Miller Philabaum & Nancy Lenches Alegret. - - 2nd ed.
p. cm.
SUMMARY: Introduction to the Sonoran Desert and the animals and
plants one might see on summer's day and night.
ISBN 0-9639215-2-5

1. Desert ecology--Sonoran Desert--Juvenile literature. 2.
Sonoran Desert--Juvenile literature. I. Alegret, Nancy Lenches.
II Title.

QH104.5.S58P45 1997   574.5'2652'097917
                              QBI96-40148

Manufactured in the United States of America

• Earth Buddies Publishing •
Tucson • Arizona

Where on Earth do you live?

Is it a rainforest, a swamp, a cave or a prairie?
Maybe you live on a coral reef, an iceberg, or a snowy mountaintop.

Maybe you live in a desert.

This book is about life in the Sonoran Desert, which lies in parts of Arizona, California, and Mexico.

Some of the plants and animals that live in this desert seem strange, or even scary. But what is funny or ugly, odd or threatening, may be what helps these creatures survive in a harsh hot environment.

Let's visit a summer day in the Sonoran Desert.

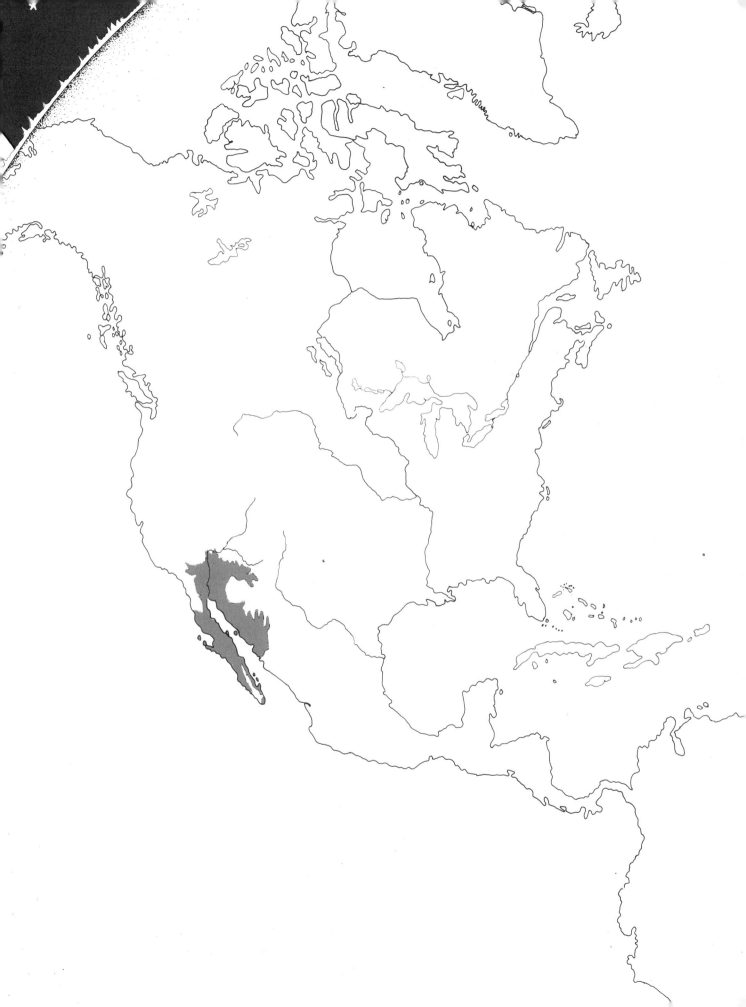

You feel the difference right away.

It's hot as a furnace and so dry your skin tickles.
The sun blazes right over your head.
You squint in the brightness and wish you had a hat.

Strange skinny plants grow out of the rocky soil.
Streambeds cut through the land, but their sandy
gravel bottoms are dry as chalk. Not a trickle of water in sight.
This dusty blistering earth is not meant for bare feet.

Nothing about this land is soft.

You notice the sky.
Big, blue, and cloudless.
The air is strangely still.

Something tells you this place is not like any other,
and you begin to wonder what lives here.

Roadrunners live here.

Roadrunners are the peculiar desert birds who would rather
run than fly. They zoom around the morning desert
　　　zig zagging
　　　　　stopping
　　　　　　　starting
　　　　　　　　dashing.

Their long tails jerk back and forth.
That's how they keep their balance.

Their toes leave an ✕ mark in the sand.
You always know who just passed, but you can never tell
which direction this desert buddy was going.

Roadrunners eat small animals such as lizards and insects,
but they also can attack rattlesnakes with their strong beaks.

When a male roadrunner likes a female
he often brings her wonderful roadrunner
gifts like

twigs

and fresh squirming lizards.

Javelina (ha-va-LEE-nah) are the desert buddies with
       coarse gray bristles,
       a snout like a pig,
       and two tusks, sharp as javelins.

That's how they got their name.
Because that's how they protect themselves if attacked by
mountain lions, coyotes or eagles.

Javelina travel in packs looking for food and water.
Each group has its own unique scent.
They identify each other by smelling instead of looking,
because their eyesight is very poor.

Although javelina eat a variety of desert plants and fruits,
they prefer the spiney pricklypear cactus.

When you walk in the Sonoran Desert, sometimes you hear the
soft grunting of contented javelina feasting on a stickery snack.

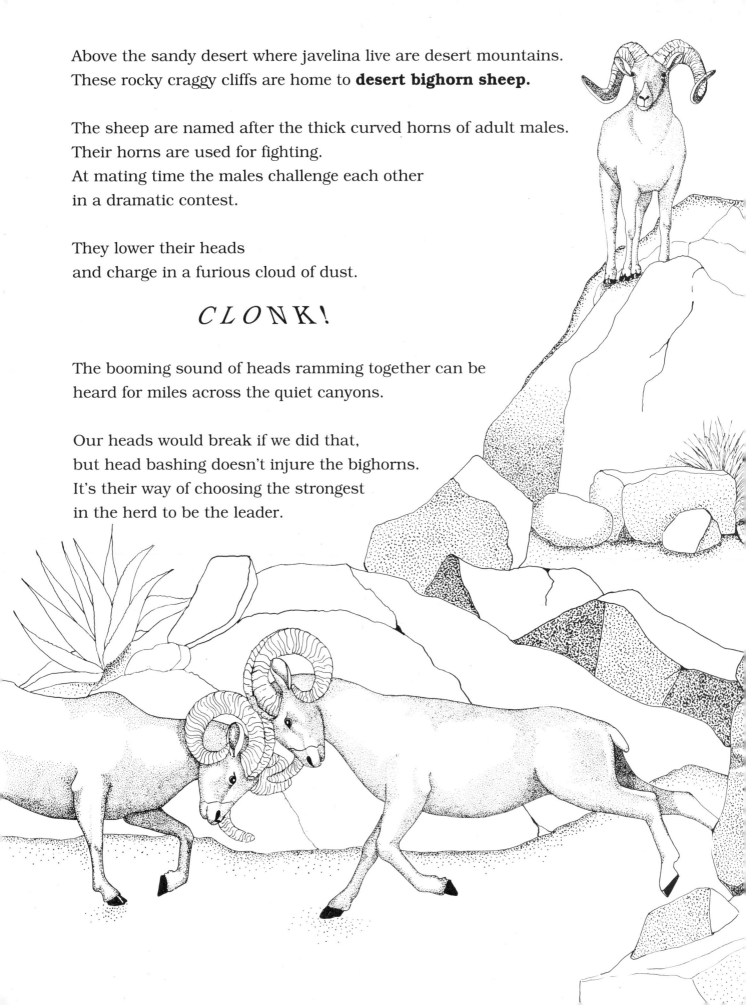

Above the sandy desert where javelina live are desert mountains.
These rocky craggy cliffs are home to **desert bighorn sheep.**

The sheep are named after the thick curved horns of adult males.
Their horns are used for fighting.
At mating time the males challenge each other
in a dramatic contest.

They lower their heads
and charge in a furious cloud of dust.

C L O N K!

The booming sound of heads ramming together can be
heard for miles across the quiet canyons.

Our heads would break if we did that,
but head bashing doesn't injure the bighorns.
It's their way of choosing the strongest
in the herd to be the leader.

Bighorn sheep eat the fruit and leaves of desert shrubs and cactus. That food is plentiful. Water is more difficult to find, and sheep must drink every few days. Sometimes all they find are small depressions in the rock called *tinajas* (teen-AH-has) which have collected rainwater and snowmelt.

Long ago the Indians of the West painted and carved thousands of pictures on rocks. Much of that ancient art includes images of desert bighorn sheep.

Seeing these pictures from the past reminds us that animals and people have shared this desert for a long time.

As the day unfolds, the still air begins to move,
and the smell of moisture slowly invades the dryness.

All the desert buddies notice.

At first it's just a breeze, bending the grasses along dry river washes.

Then the wind swells, filling the horizon with dust,
and thorny round tumbleweeds, some as big as you,
break from their roots
and go cartwheeling across the land.

The desert seems out of control.

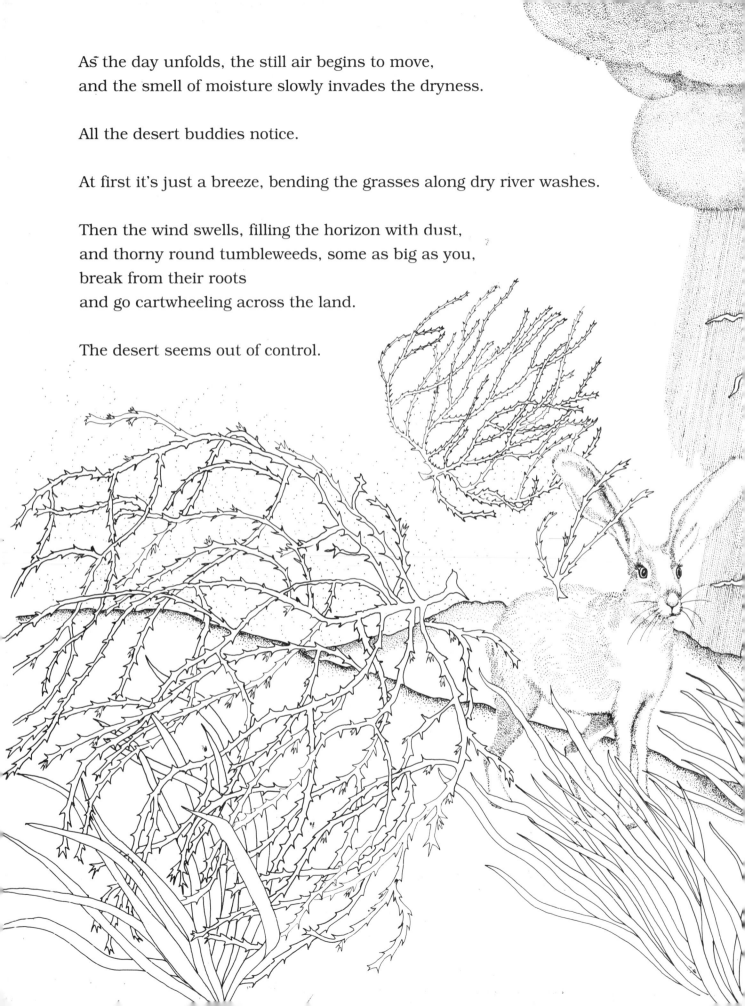

The sky turns dark as coal
and growls with deep thunder.
Then lightning strikes the restless air
again and again.

The summer rains have finally come.

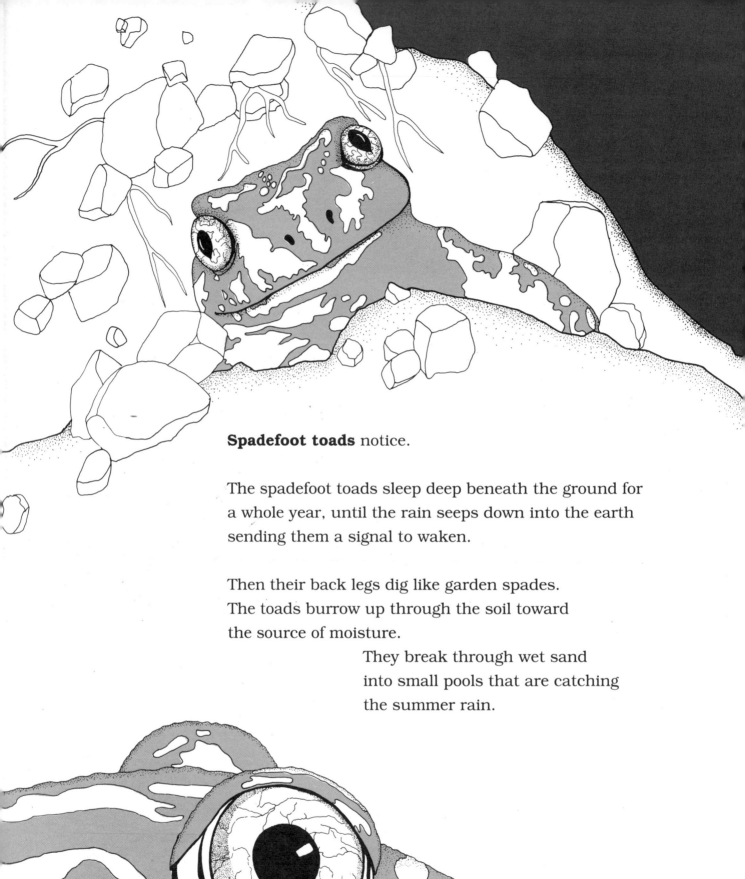

Spadefoot toads notice.

The spadefoot toads sleep deep beneath the ground for
a whole year, until the rain seeps down into the earth
sending them a signal to waken.

Then their back legs dig like garden spades.
The toads burrow up through the soil toward
the source of moisture.

> They break through wet sand
> into small pools that are catching
> the summer rain.

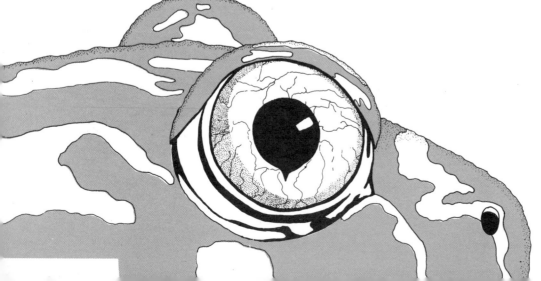

Braaaa! Braackk!

It's not a duck, a cat, or a bleating sheep.
This curious commotion is the croaking lovesong of male toads.
Soon the females leave strings of eggs in the rain puddles.

In only one day the eggs hatch into tiny tadpoles,
but they don't stay babies long. The sun is drying up their
watery home. The tadpoles quickly grow legs,
and become air-breathing toads.

But even adult toads need water to live.

When it's gone, spadefoot toads
dig down into the desert sand,
slow down their breathing, and wait.

Until the next deep rain comes.

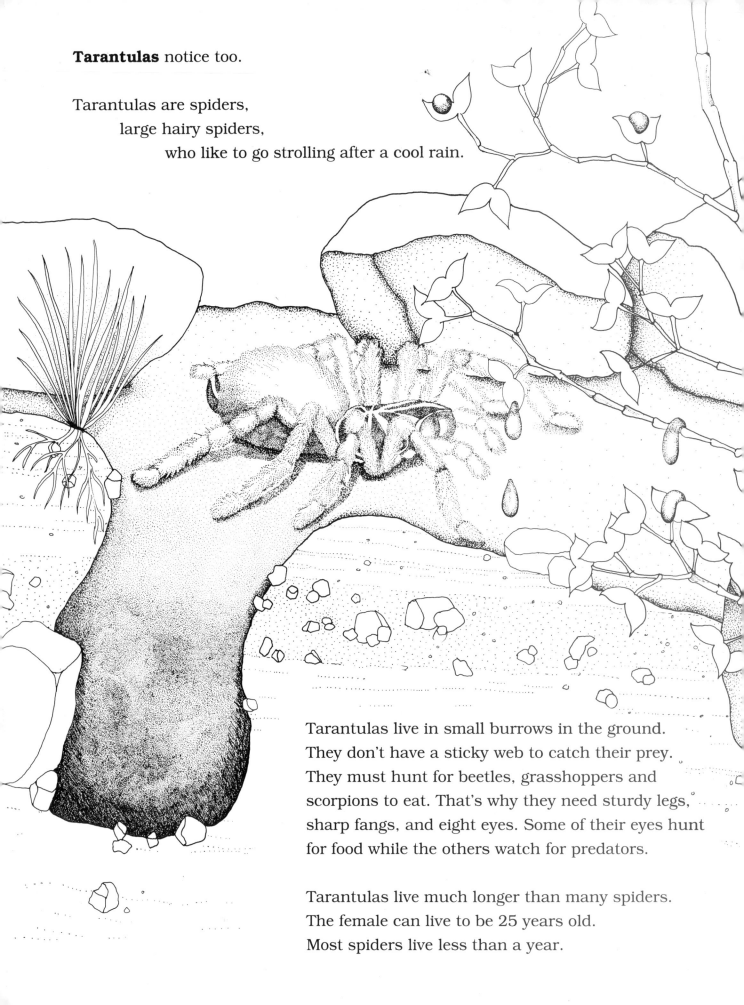

Tarantulas notice too.

Tarantulas are spiders,
　　large hairy spiders,
　　　who like to go strolling after a cool rain.

Tarantulas live in small burrows in the ground.
They don't have a sticky web to catch their prey.
They must hunt for beetles, grasshoppers and
scorpions to eat. That's why they need sturdy legs,
sharp fangs, and eight eyes. Some of their eyes hunt
for food while the others watch for predators.

Tarantulas live much longer than many spiders.
The female can live to be 25 years old.
Most spiders live less than a year.

Some people think tarantulas are scary and mean just because they are big and hairy.

Tarantulas are very gentle.

You might see one after the next rain.

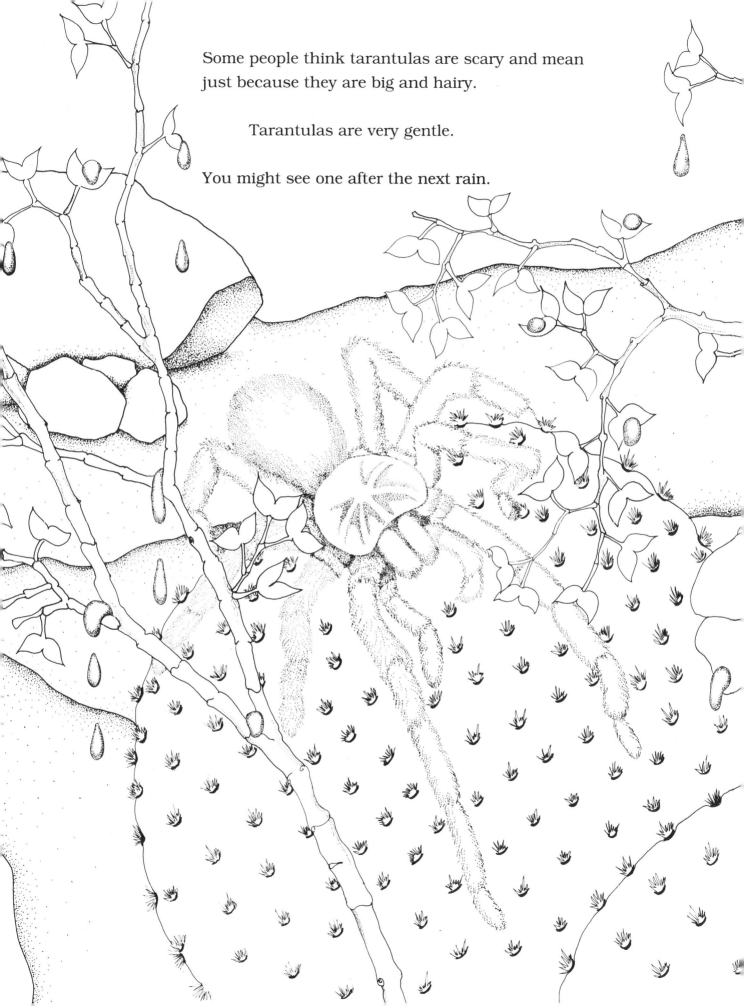

The desert smells different after a rain,
      a tangy wet smell.

It looks different too.

Water swirls through arroyos and washes.
Wildflowers sprinkle color across the land.
Everywhere you look, from the grass to the trees to the cactus,
the desert becomes gloriously green.

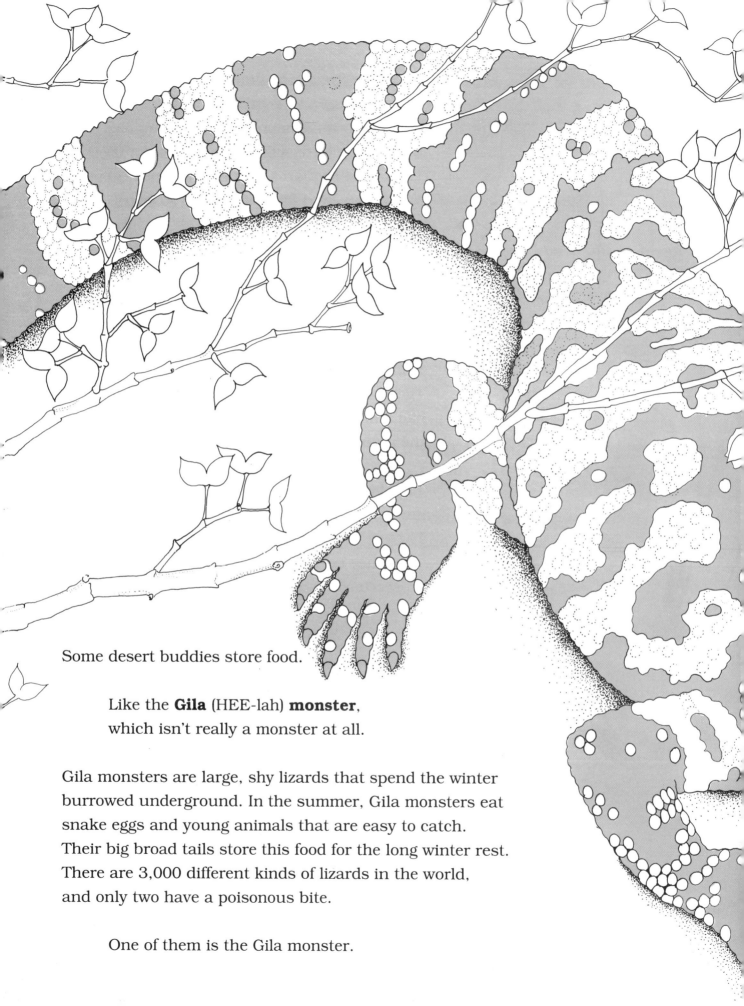

Some desert buddies store food.

Like the **Gila** (HEE-lah) **monster**,
which isn't really a monster at all.

Gila monsters are large, shy lizards that spend the winter
burrowed underground. In the summer, Gila monsters eat
snake eggs and young animals that are easy to catch.
Their big broad tails store this food for the long winter rest.
There are 3,000 different kinds of lizards in the world,
and only two have a poisonous bite.

One of them is the Gila monster.

The Gila monsters' skin looks like Indian beadwork in a beautiful orange and black pattern. They often nest under creosote, and the shade pattern of the bush camouflages their splendid skin.

These large colorful lizards live only in the Sonoran Desert, and they stay underground or out of sight most of the year.

You would be lucky to see this desert buddy.

As shadows lengthen and delicate wildflower blooms
fold up for the evening, the desert day comes to a close
in a dazzling display of color.

The western sky glows pink, purple, and red-orange
before the sun finally drops behind the mountains.

Everyone in the desert pauses for the beautiful sunset,

and all desert buddies feel relief.

Jackrabbits feel relief.

They spent the day in cool shallow pits under shady bushes,
and now they are hungry.

Jackrabbits dine on leaves, grass, and cactus. They don't have to drink water.
The water they need is in the plants they eat.

Jackrabbits have big ears and big back legs.

In cold weather, their ears lay flat to maintain body
warmth. During summer, they stand tall and pink as
body heat escapes to the air. Jacks stay cool that way.

Shhh! What was that?

When jackrabbits hear a noise their bodies freeze, but
their sensitive ears twitch and turn to find the sound.
Jackrabbits have excellent hearing.

If the sound means danger, jacks bolt in a flash,
bounding through the desert in great soaring leaps.
No desert predator can run as fast.

Jackrabbits run so fast that,
      if the weather is right,
      their speed upsets the air
      creating tiny whirling dust devils in the sand.

SzzztSzzztSzzztSzzzt

Stop.   Listen.

Could it be a **rattlesnake**?

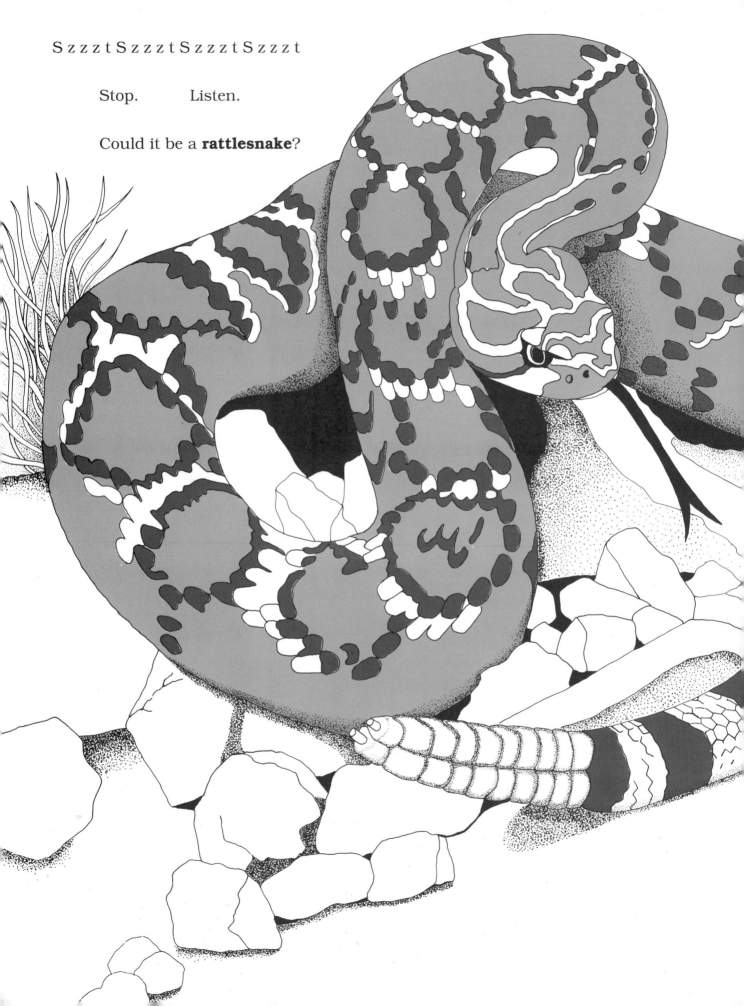

Rattlesnakes are the only snakes that have noisemakers.
When rattlesnakes sense a threat, they send a warning by vibrating the rattles
at the end of their tails. The noise is loud because the message is important.

Rattlesnake bites are dangerous.

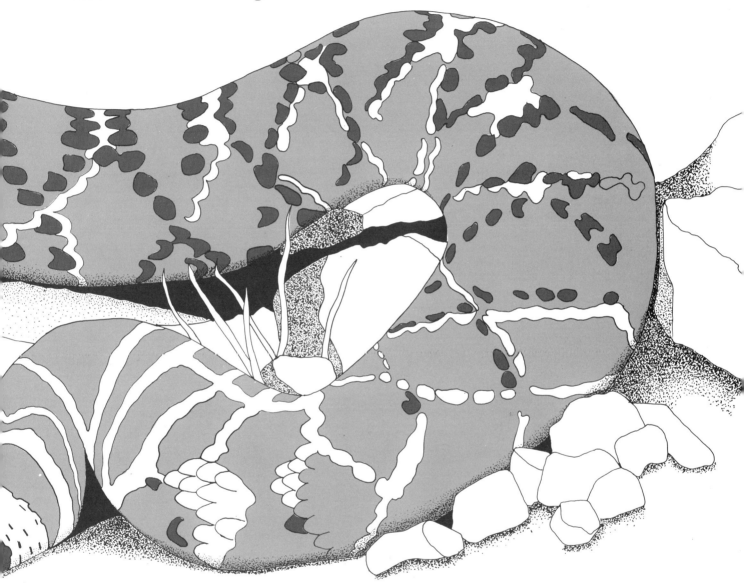

Each time a rattlesnake sheds its old skin for a new one that fits,
a section is added to its rattle. You will never shed your skin because it grows
with your body. A big rattlesnake has shed many skins.
It could have a loud rattle.

S z z z t S z z z t S z z z t S z z z t

A rattlesnake will let you know if you come too close.

All day long, lizards—big, little, collared, banded, and beaded—
dart across sand and stone.

But one kind of lizard sleeps all day.
As night falls, tiny **geckos** slowly creep
from dark daytime hideaways.

It's time to hunt some tasty crickets, termites and spiders.
Most of the food they eat will be stored in their fat tails.

But not all of it.

If a predator is after a gecko, its tail breaks off.
The flopping tail confuses the attacker while the gecko runs to safety.
Then the tail grows back.

Daytime lizards look leathery. Nighttime geckos look delicate.
Their skin is blotchy, soft and beaded.
It is so thin you can almost see inside their bodies.

They have special eyes for seeing in the dark, and the best hearing
of any lizard. They can even make sounds! Not many lizards in the
whole world can do that.

After geckos eat, you can hear them smacking their lips.
And when geckos are threatened, they squeak and chirp.

That might be worth staying up for some night.

Bats sleep during the day in a dark, quiet place.
Huddled together, they hang upside down with their
wings folded up like tiny umbrellas.

Evening brings on a great SWOOSH
as entire colonies fly out in search of food.
Only mothers and babies stay behind.

Bats fly, but they are not birds.
Bats are mammals, just like people.
They are the only mammals that fly. Their wings
consist of skin stretched between long narrow fingers.

There are a thousand different kinds of bats in the world and most of them eat insects. **Mexican free-tailed bats** live in desert caves and eat millions of moths and pesky mosquitos every night.

Another species called **lesser longnosed bats** feed on the nectar and pollen of saguaros, agaves and organ pipe cactus.

These cactus flowers open at night with tempting scents that attract bats. The bats' long noses fit perfectly into the blossoms. As they go from flower to flower, the bats spread pollen from one plant to another.

That's how new cactus plants are created.

Some people don't understand bats, and try to hurt them.

We should protect bats.
The giant saguaros need them.

Boing   Boing

Boing

Boing

It's dark in the desert when tiny **kangaroo rats** with big hind feet
begin hopping through the brush, searching for food.

They gather seeds into pouches on the outside of their cheeks. Hard,
dry seeds are about the only thing these rodents eat,
and they never need to drink!

Kangaroo rats produce water in their own bodies from the seeds and
insects they eat. You, and most other desert buddies must drink
water to live.

With so little moisture in their bodies, they can't afford to waste a bit,
so kangaroo rats stay deep in their underground burrows during the
hot day. They never lose water by sweating or panting,
like you do when you run fast.

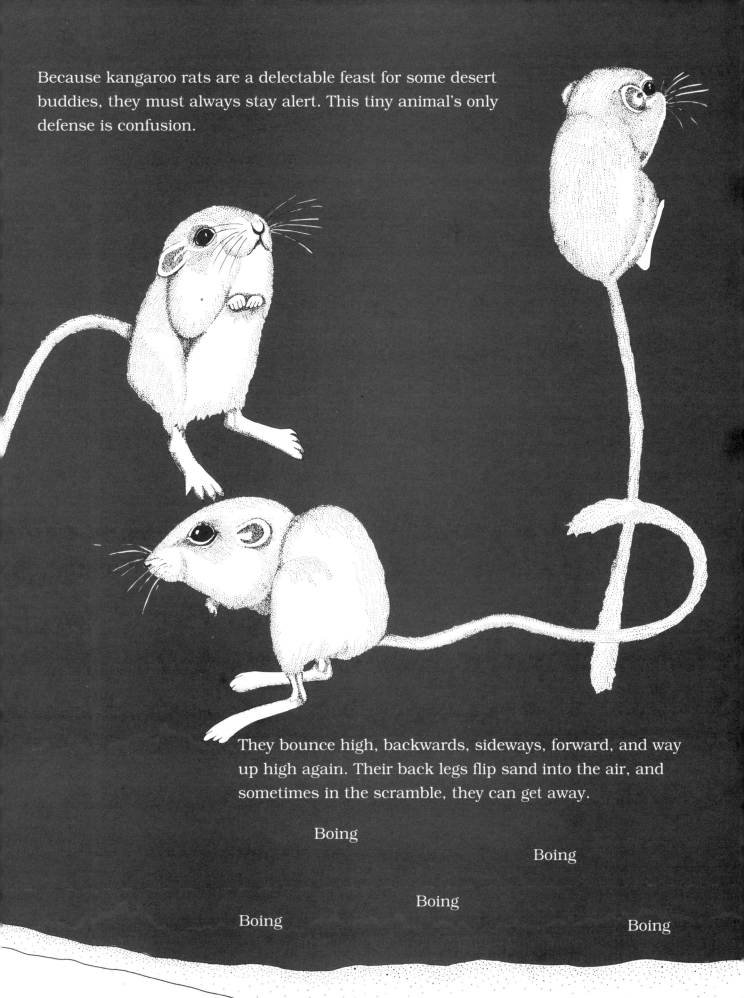

Because kangaroo rats are a delectable feast for some desert buddies, they must always stay alert. This tiny animal's only defense is confusion.

They bounce high, backwards, sideways, forward, and way up high again. Their back legs flip sand into the air, and sometimes in the scramble, they can get away.

Boing

Boing

Boing

Boing

Boing

It's the middle of the night.

A whisper of warm breeze blows the fur on the **coyote's** bushy tail.
He is hunting. He has a hungry family to feed.

The coyote must eat enough for himself and his pups. They are
too young to chew for themselves. Back at the den, he spits up
some of the food for the pups to eat.

Both parents teach their pups important coyote skills,
like how to catch a grasshopper, a mouse, and a young deer.
The playful pups learn to be quiet when danger is near, and to
avoid traps and the smell of humans. Their greatest threat is not
the wolf, cougar or eagle who need them for food.

It is man.

Coyotes can smell much better than you.
The adults teach their little ones to identify the smell
of each animal that has passed by earlier.
That's a big help in finding food and avoiding danger.

When the moon rises, coyotes turn their faces to the
starry night sky and howl into the darkness.
The pups imitate with their own squealing chorus.

They need a lot of practice.

These mysterious-sounding howls and yips have
punctured the night air for thousands of years.
Although the Indians tell many stories about howling
coyotes, no one really knows why they sing.

Perhaps the coyote song is simply celebrating the end
of one more beautiful, challenging, desert day.

• The Earth Buddies Collection •

Ask for other gifts from Earth Buddies in your local stores.
If unavailable, you can order directly from us.

DESERT BUDDIES

book	$ 7.95
official t-shirt (size L 14-16)	$11.95
book & t-shirt gift package (size L 14-16)	$17.95

OCEAN BUDDIES

book	$ 7.95
official t-shirt (size L 14-16)	$11.95
book & t-shirt gift package (size L 14-16)	$17.95

Sales tax: *Add 7% to merchandise shipped to Arizona addresses.*

Shipping & Handling: *US only on purchases totaling:*

$17.99 & under	*$3.50*
$18.00 - $39.99	*$4.00*
$40.00 & up	*$4.50*

Send your order along with a check or money order to the
address below. Please don't forget to include your shipping address.
Allow several weeks for delivery.

Enjoy!

Earth Buddies Publishing
820 South 2nd Avenue, Suite B/D
Tucson, Arizona 85701

Adios!